E WOOD A
Wood, Audrey.
Heckedy Peg

E WOOD A
Wood, Audrey.
Heckedy Peg

HECKEDY PEG

by Audrey Wood   Illustrated by Don Wood

Voyager Books
Harcourt Brace & Company

SAN DIEGO   NEW YORK   LONDON

For information about permission to
reproduce selections from this book,
please write Permissions,
Houghton Mifflin Harcourt Publishing Company
215 Park Avenue South NY NY 10003

Voyager Books is a registered trademark
of Harcourt Brace & Company.

Library of Congress Cataloging-in-Publication Data
Wood, Audrey.
Heckedy Peg.
"Voyager Books."
Summary: A mother saves her seven children from
Heckedy Peg, a witch who has changed them into
different kinds of food.
[1. Fairy tales. 2. Witches—Fiction.]
I. Wood, Don, 1945– ill. II. Title.
PZ8.W846He 1987   [E]   86-33639
ISBN 0-15-233678-8
ISBN 0-15-233679-6 pb

SCP   30 29 28 27 26
4500533555

Printed in China

The paintings in this book were done in oil on bristol board.
The text type was set in Stempel Garamond.
The display type was set in Albertus Inline.
Composition by Thompson Type, San Diego, California
Color separations by Heinz Weber, Inc., Los Angeles, California
Printed and bound by South China Printing Company Ltd.
Production supervision by Warren Wallerstein and Eileen McGlone
Design by Dalia Hartman

For Betty Smith Wood

Down the dusty roads and far away, a poor mother once lived with her seven children named Monday, Tuesday, Wednesday, Thursday, Friday, Saturday, and Sunday.

Every day before the mother went to market, her children helped with all the chores.

One morning when they were finished, the mother said, "Because you are such good children, you may ask for anything you want and I will bring it home from the market."

The children were overjoyed
and knew exactly what they wanted.

Monday asked for a tub of butter.

Thursday asked for a pot of honey.

Friday asked for a tin of salt.

Tuesday asked for a pocket knife.

Wednesday asked for a china pitcher.

Saturday asked for crackers.

And Sunday asked for a bowl
of egg pudding.

The mother kissed her children good-bye and said, "Now be careful, and remember—don't let a stranger in and don't touch fire."

The children locked the door behind her and began to play.

Before long, a witch hobbled up the road pulling a heavy cart. She rapped at the window and called out:

> "I'm Heckedy Peg.
> I've lost my leg.
> Let me in!"

"We can't," Monday, Tuesday, Wednesday, Thursday, Friday, Saturday, and Sunday called. "Mother told us not to let a stranger in."

Heckedy Peg took a pipe from her cape and stuck it in her mouth.

"Come now, sweet chickens," she called. "All I need is a light for my pipe. Bring me a burning straw."

"We can't," Monday, Tuesday, Wednesday, Thursday, Friday, Saturday, and Sunday called. "Mother told us not to touch fire."

Heckedy Peg reached in her cart and pulled out a sack.

"I'm sure your mother won't mind," she said. "Look! If you let me in and light my pipe, I'll give you this."

Leaning out the window, the children looked into the sack. They couldn't believe their eyes.

"Gold!" they cried. "For a sack of gold we'll let you in and light your pipe."

The children unlocked the door and let the witch in. They ran to the hearth and brought back burning sticks of straw to light her pipe.

But when it was lit,
Heckedy Peg threw the pipe
to the floor and shouted,
"Now I've got you!"
   And with that the witch
turned the children into food.
   Monday became bread.
   Tuesday became pie.
   Wednesday became milk.
   Thursday became porridge.
   Friday became fish.
   Saturday became cheese.
   And Sunday became
roast rib.

Heckedy Peg gathered up the food and loaded it in her cart.
Without looking back, she pulled the cart down the road,

over the bridge, through the town, across the field, and deep
into the woods to her hut.

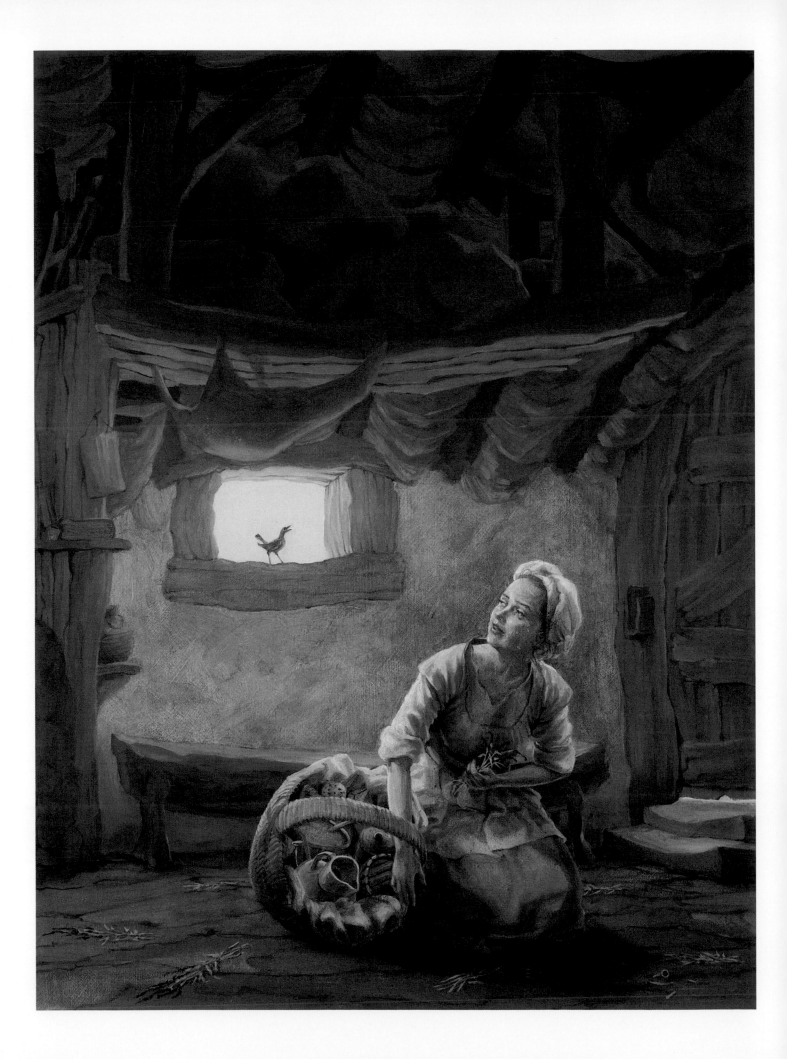

Soon the mother returned home carrying
a large basket. In it were all the things
her children wanted:
    a tub of butter for Monday,
    a pocket knife for Tuesday,
    a china pitcher for Wednesday,
    a pot of honey for Thursday,
    a tin of salt for Friday,
    crackers for Saturday,
    and a bowl of egg pudding for Sunday.
    "Monday, Tuesday, Wednesday, Thursday,
Friday, Saturday, and Sunday!" she called,
but no one answered.
    The mother found the witch's broken pipe
and burnt pieces of straw on the floor. Tears
flowed from her eyes.
    "Who has taken my children?" she cried.
    A blackbird who had seen everything took
pity on the mother and hopped down to the
windowsill.
    "Follow me!" the bird chirped.
        "It's Heckedy Peg.
        She's lost her leg.
        They let her in."
Grabbing her basket, the mother followed
the blackbird down the road, over the bridge,
through the town, across the field, and deep
into the woods to the witch's hut.

Heckedy Peg had just sat down to supper and was about to

take her first bite when she heard a loud knock at the door.

"Let me in!" the mother called. "I want my children back!"

"You can't come in!" said Heckedy Peg. "Your shoes are dirty."

"Then I'll take them off," the mother said, and so she did.

"Let me in!" the mother called. "I want my children back!"

"You can't come in!" said Heckedy Peg. "Your socks are dirty."

"Then I'll take them off," the mother said, and so she did.

"Let me in!" the mother called. "I want my children back!"

"You still can't come in!" said Heckedy Peg. "Your feet are dirty."

"Then I'll cut them off," the mother said, and she went away as if to do so. But instead, the mother hid her legs behind her and crawled back to the witch's door.

"Let me in!" the mother called. "I want my children back!"

When Heckedy Peg looked down, she thought the mother had no feet, so she let her in.

The witch pointed to the table.

"Here are your children," she said. "If you can't guess them right the first time, I'll eat them for my supper."

Keeping her feet tucked beneath her, the mother crawled to the table. How would she ever guess which food was which child?

In despair, the mother looked in her basket. *Here are the things my children wanted*, she thought, *and now they will never have them.*

"Hurry!" said the witch, "I'm hungry."

The mother looked at the food on the table.

"Speak up!" said the witch. "My supper grows cold."

Suddenly the mother knew what to do. Taking the things from her basket, she said, "I know my children by what they want."

"Bread wants butter. That's Monday.

"Pie wants knife. That's Tuesday.

"Milk wants pitcher. That's Wednesday.

"Porridge wants honey. That's Thursday.

"Fish wants salt. That's Friday.

"Cheese wants crackers. That's Saturday.

"And roast rib wants egg pudding. That's Sunday."

Quick as a wink, the children turned back into themselves.

They hugged and kissed their mother, then hugged and kissed each other.

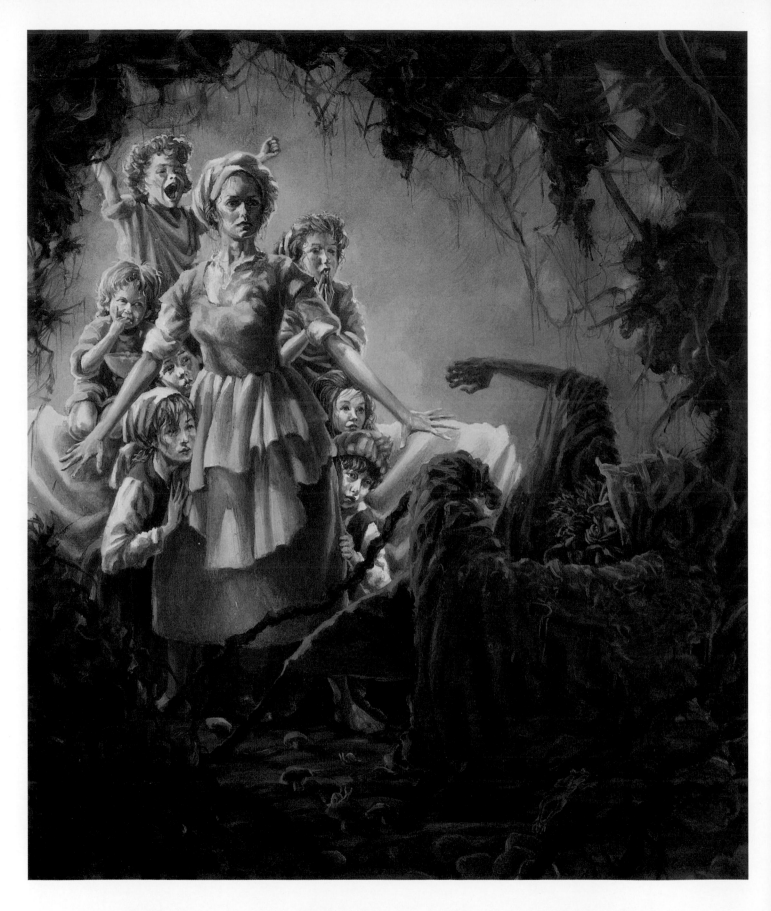

Jumping to her feet, the mother cried, "I've got my children back, Heckedy Peg. Now you'll be sorry you ever took them!"

She chased the witch around the hut, out of the woods, across the field, through the town, and onto the bridge.

And Heckedy Peg jumped off the bridge and was never seen again.